Dear Parents and Educators,

Welcome to Penguin Young Readers! As parents and educators, you know that each child develops at his or her own pace—in terms of speech, critical thinking, and, of course, reading. Penguin Young Readers recognizes this fact. As a result, each Penguin Young Readers book is assigned a traditional easy-to-read level (1–4) as well as a Guided Reading Level (A–P). Both of these systems will help you choose the right book for your child. Please refer to the back of each book for specific leveling information. Penguin Young Readers features esteemed authors and illustrators, stories about favorite characters, fascinating nonfiction, and more!

Happy Birthday, Good Knight

LEVEL 3

GUIDED READING LEVEL J

This book is perfect for a **Transitional Reader** who:
- can read multisyllable and compound words;
- can read words with prefixes and suffixes;
- is able to identify story elements (beginning, middle, end, plot, setting, characters, problem, solution); and
- can understand different points of view.

Here are some **activities** you can do during and after reading this book:
- Problem/Solution: In this story, the three little dragons need to get a birthday gift, but they don't have any money. That is the problem. Discuss the solution to this problem. How does the Knight help them?
- Creative Writing: If you were to throw a birthday party for the Good Knight, what would you do? Write a paragraph that describes the party. What activities would you plan? What kind of presents would you give him? Remember that the best gifts of all are those given from your heart and your hand, just as the Good Knight says!

Remember, sharing the love of reading with a child is the best gift you can give!

—Bonnie Bader, EdM
Penguin Young Readers program

*Penguin Young Readers are leveled by independent reviewers applying the standards developed by Irene Fountas and Gay Su Pinnell in *Matching Books to Readers: Using Leveled Books in Guided Reading*, Heinemann, 1999.

For J.B. III—SMT

For Maggie, with thanks—JP

PENGUIN YOUNG READERS
Published by the Penguin Group
Penguin Group (USA) LLC, 375 Hudson Street, New York, New York 10014, USA

USA | Canada | UK | Ireland | Australia | New Zealand | India | South Africa | China

penguin.com
A Penguin Random House Company

 First published in 2006 by Dutton Children's Books, an imprint of Penguin Group (USA) LLC. Published in 2014 by Penguin Young Readers, an imprint of Penguin Group (USA) LLC, 345 Hudson Street, New York, New York 10014. Manufactured in China.

The Library of Congress has catalogued the Dutton edition under the following Control Number: 2005009592

ISBN 978-0-448-46374-2

10 9 8 7 6 5 4 3

PENGUIN YOUNG READERS

LEVEL 3
TRANSITIONAL READER

Happy Birthday, Good Knight

by Shelley Moore Thomas
pictures by Jennifer Plecas

Penguin Young Readers
An Imprint of Penguin Group (USA) LLC

The sun was rising
over the deep, dark forest.
Inside a cozy cave there
lived three little dragons.
They were talking with their
friend the Good Knight.

“We have a problem,” said the first dragon.

“We need to get a birthday gift,” said the second dragon.

“For someone very special,” said the third dragon.

"But we don't have any money.
What can we do?"
asked all three dragons.
The Good Knight thought and
thought.
"Aha!" he said. "Methinks I know."

“The most special gifts
do not come from a store.
They come from our hearts
and our hands, nothing more,”
said the Good Knight.
“What does that mean?”
asked all three dragons.

“The best gifts are the ones
we make ourselves,”
said the Good Knight.
“Will you help us? Please?”
asked the dragons.
The Good Knight did not
know what to think.

But he was a good knight.

"Come with me," he said.

The Good Knight

hitched up the cart.

The dragons got in.

He jumped on his horse.

Clippety-clop. Clippety-clop.

They went through the deep, dark

forest to the Good Knight's

crumbly, tumbly tower.

"We will make a cake,"
said the Good Knight.
"Everybody loves cake!"

In the Good Knight's kitchen,
the work began.
The dragons made a double-layer,
double-chocolate, double-swirl cake
with sparkly sprinkles on top.
At least they tried to.

But three little dragons
in one little kitchen can make
one big mess.
"I don't believe this!"
said the Good Knight.
There was flour on the ceiling,
sugar on the chairs, cake batter
on the floor, and sprinkles
everywhere.

"This is a wreck!"
cried the Good Knight.

He got the clean-up buckets

and soapy soapsuds.

He got the brooms
and brushes.

The dragons scrubbed the ceiling.

Scrubby, scrubby, scrubby.

The dragons swept the floor.

Swish, swish, swish.

They even washed the seats
of the chairs.
Brush-a, brush-a, brush-a.

They cleaned until the kitchen was

“We still have a problem,”
said the dragons.
“We still don’t have a birthday
gift for someone very special.”
And they began to cry drippy,
droppy dragon tears.

The Good Knight did not know what to think.
But he was a good knight.
So he came up with a new idea.
"Don't cry, good dragons,"
said the Good Knight.
"We will make a birthday card.
Everybody loves birthday cards!"

In the Good Knight's study,
the work began.
The little dragons made a giant
pop-up birthday card
with shimmery, glimmery rainbows.
At least they tried to.

But three little dragons
in one little study can
make one big mess.

“I don’t believe this!”
cried the Good Knight.

There was paint on the ceiling,
glue on the chairs, paper on the
floor, and glitter everywhere.
And the pop-up card was glued shut.
“This is a ruin!”
cried the Good Knight.
He got the clean-up buckets
and soapy soapsuds.
He got the brooms
and brushes.

The dragons scrubbed the ceiling.

Scrubby, scrubby, scrubby.

The dragons swept the floor.

Swish, swish, swish.

They even washed the seats
of the chairs.
Brush-a, brush-a, brush-a.

They cleaned unil the study was

"We still don't have a birthday gift
for someone very special,"
said the dragons.
And they began to cry
drippy, droppy dragon tears.
The Good Knight did not
know what to think.

But he was a good knight.

And he got another good idea.

"We will put on a magic show.

Everybody loves magic!" he said.

In the Good Knight's sitting room,

the work began.

The dragons planned a flashy,
splashy magic show with balloon
animals, bright colored streamers,
and birds that flew away.
At least they tried to.

But three little dragons
in one little sitting room
can make one big mess.

“I don’t believe this!”
cried the Good Knight.
There were feathers on the
ceiling, streamers on the chairs,
bits of paper on the floor, and
popped balloons everywhere.
“This is a disaster!” he cried.
He got the clean-up buckets
and soapy soapsuds.
He got the brooms and brushes.

The dragons scrubbed the ceiling.

Scrubby, scrubby, scrubby.

The dragons swept the floor.

Swish, swish, swish.

They even washed the seats
of the chairs.
Brush-a, brush-a, brush-a.

They cleaned until the
sitting room was

C-L-E-A-N.

The Good Knight sat down
at his little kitchen table.
It was very late.
He was very tired.
The clock struck midnight.
"Oh no!" cried the little dragons.
"Now it is too late!"
The dragons began to cry
drippy, droppy dragon tears.
"Today was your birthday.
We wanted the birthday gift
for you.
Now it is too late,"
said the dragons.

The Good Knight looked
at his calendar.
Yes, indeed, it was his birthday.
He began to smile.
Then he giggled and laughed.
"You have given me the best gift
there is," he said.

The dragons did not know
what to think.
"We did not make a cake or a card
or a magic show.
We only made big, fat messes,"
they said.

"You made something else.
You made me laugh!"
said the Good Knight.
"The gift of laughter
is the best gift there is!"
The dragons thought of
the big, fat messes.

They began to smile.
They giggled and laughed.
They laughed until the
drippy, droppy dragon tears
were all gone.

"Yes, little dragons.
I will never forget this day,"
said the Good Knight.

Then the Good Knight
and the three little dragons
ate the burnt cake.

The Good Knight opened his sticky, gluey card.

The dragons did a magic trick.

Then the dragons began to sing:

“Happy birthday to you.

Happy birthday to you.

Happy birthday, Good Knight.

Happy birthday to you!”

“Thank you, good dragons,”
said the Good Knight.
“It was a good birthday.”